A Yuletide Wish
Poems and Stories
for the Extended Holiday Season

Night Wolf Publications

A Yuletide Wish

Poems and Stories
for the Extended Holiday Season

ISBN 978-09866406-4-3

Night Wolf Publications
www.nightwolfpublications.com

First Edition: 2010

Dedication
To our test readers

Acknowledgments
The publishers would like to thank the authors who took the time to submit their precious words and ideas to make this holiday compilation such a pleasant and quality product. We also thank Aluska Bissaro and Alisha Moreland for their help putting our best foot forward with a lovely cover.

A Note from the Editor

Dear Reader,

From the first hint of chill when red and golden leaves flutter down and kids pray for snow days, people feel excitement building inside them. Christmas is coming! There's candy to scarf down from Halloween night. There are pies to bake for a Thanksgiving gathering fit for a king. There's an eight-night festival of lights for families and friends. There's the wrapping and tree-trimming and finding just the right cookies to leave out for Santa as we build up to Christmas morning. To top the season off, we ring in a new year with a world-wide community.

At a time when too many things in the world require grim headlines, it's a joy to bring you this compilation of happy-ending, holiday stories that you can pick up for a pick-me-up at any time of the year. I hope you use this book as a good excuse to sit down with family and a round of hot cocoa—maybe two. May the children's stories, young adult stories, and the sweet holiday romances bring you smiles...and a few chuckles. Everything in this book has been vetted to bring you a clean, family-friendly cannon of new holiday favorites. May all your yuletide wishes come true.

I wish you a very merry Christmas and a beautiful new year,
Sandy Lender

Table of Contents

Black-capped Chickadee in WinterFront Cover

Night Wolf Publications

Children's Stories

Baby in the Manger
by Barbara Bockman

Mrs. Swallow stood at the entrance of the barn and felt the cool autumn wind ruffle her feathers. Orange and brown leaves swirled at her feet. She looked up to see a V-pattern of geese flying over the farm.

"Honk! Honk! Honk!" called the geese.

Mr. Swallow flew down from the nest in the barn rafters. "What a racket!" he said. "But they have the right idea. Cold weather is coming on."

"Yes," Mrs. Swallow shivered. "It's time to fly south."

They entered the barn and flew up to their nest, which clung to a rough board plank close to the ceiling. Mrs. Swallow looked inside. "Our nest is empty."

"We raised two good broods this year." Mr. Swallow's forked tail swished with pride. "They've already flown away. Are you ready to go?"

Mrs. Swallow nodded her head and spread her glossy blue-black wings. Before she could take off, she heard a faint screeching from below. "What was that?" she asked.

Their neighbor Mr. Owl opened his big eyes. "Whooo woke me up?"

The owl and both swallows flew down and perched on the edge of the cow's manger. The peeping cry was coming from under the hay. Mrs. Cow shuffled sideways, and the birds pushed aside the hay.

"Funny looking," Mr. Swallow said. "It looks like a mouse."

"But it has wings," Mrs. Swallow said.

"Funny looking wings," he insisted.

"It's a baby bat," Mr. Owl announced.

"Is he hurt?" Mr. Swallow asked.

"Just dazed, I think," Mrs. Cow mooed.

"We have to help him," Mrs. Swallow said. "Mrs. Cow, may we build the baby a nest in your manger?"

"Of course," Mrs. Cow said.

The swallows brought in globs of mud and fashioned a nest onto the inside of the feedbox. Pieces of straw mixed into the mud helped hold the nest together.

"Bats don't live in mud cups," Mr. Owl said.

"It's the only kind of nest we know how to build," Mr. Swallow said.

When the nest was dry, all the mice in the barn gathered on the edge of the manger. "We'll line the nest with bits of our fur," Father Mouse offered.

"Come, children," Mother Mouse said. "Let me inspect you first—see if you're clean."

The mouse children giggled as they pulled fur from each other's tummies. Marvin Mouse said, "That tickles," and scrunched his elbows into his sides.

Soon the nest was finished and cozy with mouse fur. The Swallows scooted the baby bat into it.

Mrs. Cow said, "This has to be the first time a baby bat was raised in a swallow nest."

"Whooo would have thought?" Mr. Owl asked.

"How shall we feed him?" Mrs. Swallow asked. "He's too small for insects."

"There aren't many insects this time of year," her husband reminded her. "I could enjoy a big fat mosquito myself."

"I'll provide him with milk," Mrs. Cow offered.

For several days, Mr. and Mrs. Swallow took care of the baby bat, one parent always staying awake through the night because the baby slept during the day. Each morning Mrs. Swallow sang her warbling lullaby as she put the baby to sleep. And Mrs. Cow gave him milk.

One night, the birds and cow were disturbed by noisy flapping wings. The baby bat jumped up and flew. "Wheee!" he said.

The next morning, Mr. Swallow yawned big. "The baby kept me up half the night."

"Where is he?" Mrs. Swallow sounded alarmed.

"Where would he be?" asked Mr. Owl, pointing his curved beak upward.

Mrs. Swallow found the baby hanging upside down from one of the barn rafters. "He's strong enough to fly South with us now."

The baby bat woke up and saw Mrs. Swallow. "Mama," he said.

"Oh, he thinks he's a swallow." She sounded both worried and pleased.

"We'll take care of him through the winter and bring him back here in the spring," Mr. Swallow said. "Then he can meet his real parents."

"His *other* parents, you mean," Mrs. Swallow said.

"It won't be the same without you," Mrs. Cow said. "But I know it's best that you be on your way. You'll be able to feast on lots of bugs at Christmastime in the South."

"Watch out for hawks," Mr. Owl advised.

Mr. and Mrs. Swallow let the baby bat sleep throughout the day. As the peaceful evening settled over the barnyard, all of the mice lined up in front of the open door. Streaks of red and yellow sky shown through the bare branches of the trees while the sun sank lower and lower. As soon as the last rays of light were gone, the baby bat awoke.

"Time for us to head south," Mr. Swallow told him. "Plenty of insects for us to catch on the wing down there."

"Follow us, Baby," Mrs. Swallow said, leading the way.

The baby bat swooped out of the barn, skimming the heads of the mice in the mouse family. "Bye," he called to his friends.

"We'll miss you," the mice children squeaked.

"Have a nice trip," Father Mouse said.

"Come back inside, children." Mother Mouse's fur spiked. "That wind is cold."

Mr. Owl flew out and perched on a tree limb. He watched the shape of the birds and the bat grow smaller and smaller in the distance. Snow began to fall. Christmas was in the air.

Pumpkin Tea
by Margaret Fieland

Pumpkins in a field, one night
grew long legs, began to fight.
Scarecrow, when he wandered by,
fashioned pumpkins into pie,

summoned eager dogs and cats.
Dogs wore gloves, cats wore hats.
They ate pumpkin pies for tea.
I wish they had invited me.

Leah the Hummingbird
by Liath McTire

At 2:17 p.m. on Christmas Eve, Leah the Hummingbird flew into the keep, high above the horse gate. Darting lower, she flew across the snow-covered bailey, over the heads of the hunting hounds, and through an open window into the warm keep kitchen. All of the keep drudges, which included the lord and lady of the keep, for everyone worked in this keep, were hard at work preparing the meal to celebrate the return of the sun.

Leah had always been happy flying in the sun. The lord and lady were not all that fond of the sun, but they knew that all seasons come in their own appointed time. Besides, celebrating is fun, particularly when winter has been dark and cold.

Leah flew around the kitchen, flying just above the heads of the lord and lady, but they were so busy, they did not notice her. Leah was not disturbed by not being noticed. She was hungry. The kitchen was warm and full of color. Color could mean food, food that she needed. Leah examined each and every color but could find no food.

While Leah examined the colors, the lady of the keep looked up from kneading her dough. There was Leah hovering just over her head.

"Oh look, my lord, a hummingbird has come to visit. She must have flown a very long way."

The lord of the keep looked at Leah and said, "How odd. 'Tis not the season for hummingbirds. She must be lost."

Leah took this bit of information to mean there were correct seasons for birds like her and there

13

were incorrect seasons. Just now she was too hungry and not the least concerned whether or not she was in season. She was on the hunt for food and could find none in the kitchen. She flew to the next room.

One of the drudges, Mistress Very Tall Spiked Hat, opened the pantry door to find more cinnamon and in flew Leah. The pantry room was small and filled with shelves and drawers and cubbyholes. Everywhere jars and boxes and ropes of not hummingbird food were stacked, stored, or hung from the ceiling. On top of a box on the very top shelf sat Itty Bitty Mouse.

Itty Bitty Mouse squeaked to Leah, "Won't you come and join me? There's always plenty to eat here and most of it is very good."

Leah hovered over the food Itty Bitty Mouse was nibbling, "I wish I could, Itty Bitty Mouse. But all your food is all the wrong color and probably wouldn't be good for me." Leah flew lower to hover face to face with Itty Bitty. "Thank you for your invitation. You're a gentleman mouse."

The next room was for dining. Although the red curtains were just the right color for Leah she could not eat curtains. Throughout the dining hall there were tables and chairs and settings for the many expected guests. On the walls hung brightly colored paintings and she examined each one carefully, but there was no food.

On the buffet in the dining hall lay Old Fat Cat, who was once Mighty Hunter though now she was happy to be retired. She eyed Leah with an almost friendly, but not too friendly, eye. At one time, in her younger days, Leah would have been a tasty appetizer for Mighty Hunter. Now,

Old Fat Cat was well fed and lazy, and Leah was only a passing curiosity.

Old Fat Cat thought to Leah, "Are you hungry, Fleet Flyer? If you wait till dinner is served you can sit on the lap of the lord of the keep and he will slip you tidbits."

Leah considered that while eyeing Old Fat Cat a bit warily, "No, thank you, Old Fat Cat. I don't think I do sitting-on-laps very well."

Leah flew to the next room and that room was lined with books. On the stuffed couch in the library sat Really Big Dog. Really Big Dog watched Leah, and the enthusiasm and energy of his thoughts almost knocked Leah out of the air.

"Hiya, bird! Wanna wrestle with me?"

"Oh, no, thank you, Really Big Dog. I'm very hungry."

Leah flew from book to book. She saw lots of colors, but the colors were all wrong, and there was no food behind any of them.

"Bird, you're in the wrong room! If you're hungry, go beg in the kitchen. The lady of the keep is always good for a tasty scrap or two."

"No, thank you, Really Big Dog. I flew through the kitchen and there is no food for me there."

Leah flew on. Now she was beginning to feel faint and a little weak. She had to find food soon or she would be in a lot of trouble. The next room was the grand ballroom. It was so big, Leah felt extra small. She had never felt small when she was flying in the trees outside the keep.

The grand ballroom was filled with tables and chairs, and at one end of the ballroom stood a stage for performers. In the center of the ballroom stood a very tall Christmas tree that reached almost to the roof.

Leah hoped there was food on the tree because right now, the tree seemed about as far as her energy would take her. As she got closer, Leah saw the Christmas tree was hung with big, bright, red globes that shimmered with warm and friendly magic. Surrounding each globe was the sense of food. Leah was ecstatic. She was very, very happy, and flew forward as fast as her little wings could carry her. That was pretty fast.

The globes were food! They were glorious, energizing, red food. Leah drank and drank until she was really, really full. Then the lady of the keep stepped toward Leah and held out a finger for Leah to sit on. Leah decided to sit and rest on the lady's finger.

The lord of the keep said, "Welcome to our keep, Miss Hummingbird. The sun may be returning, but he takes his time. The weather outside is much too cold for such a wee bird as you. Come stay with us in our warm keep, and this can be your home, too, until spring brings back the warmth and food is plentiful for you."

And that is what Leah the Hummingbird did.

Christmas Eve Essay
by Farida Samerkhanova

Yesterday night we all went to school for the Christmas concert. "We" is my whole family— my mother, my grandmother, my great grandmother, my great uncle and my aunt. She is my aunt, but I call her my sister, as she is just nineteen. I am in grade four. Our class performed two songs. Rehearsing was fun, but singing on stage was still more fun. I could see that some of my friends felt very shy on stage. I did not. I am used to being on stage. I dance Ukrainian dances and we sometimes perform on stage in front of hundreds of people.

First we sang *I Want a Hippopotamus for Christmas*. I like the song. All of us had a stuffed animal in our hands. I had a frog. I picked it because it reminds me of summer. Lucy had a hippopotamus, and she would always step forward and show it to the audience, raising her hand with the toy. I know that every time Lucy stepped forward, my grandmother was nervous, because she was taking pictures of me and Lucy screened me from the camera every time we sang the refrain, which was the funniest part of the performance. My grandmother is crazy about taking pictures. She has her camera ready wherever we go. The Christmas concert is important for her, for sure. She wants to take photos of every moment of my life. I think this is because she loves me so much. I appreciate it, but sometimes it is really annoying.

She loves me and takes care of me. She even knits sweaters and pullovers for me. I sang the hippopotamus song in the white pullover that she

17

made a couple of years ago. It must have been too big for me when I started wearing it, because now it fits me okay.

The second song was a nice and serious one called *Silent Night*. It is not a song about Santa and gifts. It is about the baby Jesus. I played the role of Joseph, and Tanya, my classmate, was Maria, which is another name for Mary. She was in a white robe, with a white kerchief on her head. I think she looked very pretty as Maria. Her eyes sparkled and she looked with great love at the tiny bundle that lay between her and me. That was a small doll in cloths, which we used to be the baby Jesus. I had a thick grey robe on. It was Thomas' robe. He brought it from home especially for me. It was a regular bathrobe, but on stage with other parts, it looked like a real garment of those days. I liked my costume.

Last year I also had a costume that looked like the Middle East clothes of the beginning of the new era. My grandmother put a white square kerchief on my head and fixed it with a twisted thick rope. I had a big size white T-shirt on with a rope on my waist. And my pants were my karate pants, which looked just right in combination with the other pieces. I am sure my grandmother has pictures of last year's costume, too.

I liked the concert and I liked sitting in front of all the classmates with Tanya and playing the part of Joseph. Yesterday I had a crush on Tanya, I think. It did not last long, no more than three hours. It was over by the time I came home, but I should admit it felt so good.

Today is a special day. It is Christmas Eve. I always wake up very early on this day. I can feel tranquility and happiness. I stand looking out of the window. It is snowing. The front yard is all white: the grass, the driveway, the bushes and the cars. It looks like Russia. I came to Canada when I was four, but I still remember winter back there. There is so much snow there. I liked to toboggan, to ski, to snowboard, and to skate. I still like it, but here it's all different: there is less snow, artificial ice, and safety helmets. Back in Russia it is always frost, open air, and more risk. I like both—Canada and Russia. Canada is my country now, and Russia is the country where I was born.

Everyone is still sleeping. Or pretend to be sleeping. Maybe they all stay in their bedrooms, waiting for me to go to the washroom to pee. When they hear me turning on the water or flushing the toilet they will all get out to their bedrooms and start hugging me and kissing. I do not mind. I love them all and they have to express their love for me somehow.

Before I go out of my bedroom I will turn away from the window and look at the chair beside my bed. No matter how hard I try to stay awake at night and watch, the chair manages to appear beside my bed when I do not see it coming. My great grandmother says that a magician brings it in. I think it is her or my grandmother who brings the chair in while I am sleeping. It is a special chair on this special day. It is full of presents, postcards and tiny treasures. All the things are placed on top of a very nice and very clean cotton napkin. It is a tradition. And I always find a chocolate and an apple on the chair. All other things may vary, but the napkin, the chocolate and the apple come to me year after year, even when I was in Russia.

It is my birthday. I am nine. I am big now. It feels good. I am just ten years younger than my aunt. Soon I will be an adult and I can go to work, marry, and have kids. I will drive a Hummer and have a great job. My great grandmother will baby-sit with my children. I want to have many children, like my teacher Mrs. G. She has a big daughter and her son was born when I was in grade one.

I go to the chair. I still wonder who brought it in and when. Nice greeting cards. I know exactly who wrote them, because they all say "To my grandson" or "To my nephew." On the chair I find everything I dreamed of: a new Nintendo DS, several cartridges, all Indiana Jones Lego sets that I wanted. Sweets, chocolates, and other presents and treats. What could not fit on the chair was beside the chair.

Under the chair there is a parcel, unpacked. I know it is from my uncle in Russia. Every year he sends me a parcel for my birthday. My uncle loves me and I love him. Only he lives in Russia. The rest of my family lives here in Toronto. He asked permission to come to visit us many times, but his applications were refused. I do not understand why he cannot come here and visit me. I miss him. I speak to him over Skype, but it only makes me sad, as I want to touch him, hug him, and share a piece of my birthday cake with him. It hurts, I should say. I can imagine how hard it is for my grandmother not to be able to see her son. He is a TV host over there. He is a celebrity. But even if he were not, I would love him anyway. I tear off the wrapping paper and find "Peril in Peru" Lego. How did he know I wanted this? I feel like crying. I love my uncle so much.

I love them all, especially my great uncle, who is my best friend. And my mom, because she is my mom. And my great grandmother, because she is always with me, day and night, except for the time when I am at school and except for the time when I was here in Canada and she was still back in Russia. But she was here by the time I was five. She plays soccer with me and Monopoly too; she does Lego with me and cooks for me. I am nine and she is seventy-nine.

I know it is just the beginning of the most special day. We'll have a big program today and tomorrow. We'll have a big Christmas dinner. I will have my birthday cake and make a wish. We'll have fun in the daytime with my friends—my mom always makes a nice party on this day. This year I am having a party at the LazerQuest. I invited boys from my class and also two girls—Sophie and Lucy. Last year I invited Pameli, but she has left for her home country, Mexico, and I cannot invite her this year. My best friend Ignas will come with his little brother Augustas. When I first met Augustas he was seven months old. Now he is a big boy, and we always take him to play with us.

Tomorrow morning I will find more presents. These will be from Santa. On the New Year eve I will have still more presents from Grandfather Frost from Russia. I do love this time of the year.

When I get out of the bathroom, all my family is waiting outside. They smile, say "happy birthday," kiss me, and hug me. I smile. Everyone is happy. For sure, this is a special day. But it is not about gifts and treats. The main thing for me is to feel how much my folks love me and to realize that I am getting bigger, smarter, and happier.

21

Young Adult Stories

A Birdie Wonderland
by Barbara, Raye, and Louis

Toy bells ring, are you listenin?
In the cage, parrots glistenin'
A beautiful sight, under full-spectrum light
Living in a birdie wonderland

Renovate and we could build a bird room
And pretend it really was for us
Central heat and air, humidifier
No carpet to collect the birdie dust!

Evening comes, beaks start grinding
Swings or tents, they start finding
You'll hear them all say, as you tip-toe away
"Nite-nite" from the birds in wonderland.

The China Doll
by R.P. Rebel

I've always loved the Christmas season and this year's promised to be very special. My new bride, Amy, and I left Pennsylvania in the Spring of 1882 and traveled by Conestoga wagon to Independence, Missouri, to start our new life together. The trip itself was long and arduous, but peaceful enough. Back East we had heard stories of wagon trains being wiped out by savage Indians, but the Lord was with us and we never saw one.

Upon arriving in Independence I opened my first store. I prided myself on the quality of goods I carried. Nothing but the best bolts of cloths, china, cooking pots, and, at my wife's insistence, the latest in women's fashions. In addition, I also carried a fine selection of toys for the children. It was the finest store in town, if I do say so myself, and it bore my name, Ritter's Mercantile.

It was the week before Christmas and business was bustling. The morning rush was over and I attended to the final details of my window display. I had toy boats, trains, the ever popular sled as well as a bat and ball for the boys. For the girls, I had a vast array of dolls. Everything from the standard rag doll to the jewel of the display, a beautiful china doll all the way from England.

Finished, I went outside to admire my handiwork. That's when I first saw her. A little moppet of no more than four. Mousy brown hair peeked out from under her sun-faded bonnet. Her brown eyes, wide as saucers, firmly fixed on the china doll in my window. I felt a bit sorry for her

23

as I knew there was no way her parents could afford that beauty. There was only one family in all of Independence, the Patterson's, that could afford her. George Patterson owned the largest bank in town and also happened to have three young daughters. When I ordered the doll, it was with him in mind. I knew he would buy it for one of his girls.

Freezing in the cold winter air, I started back inside when I felt a plucking at my sleeve.

"Excuse me, sir," the moppet said. "How much for the pretty doll?"

"That is a very expensive doll, Miss. She costs five dollars," I said, expecting she would be disappointed and leave. Instead, she dug deep into the pocket of her patched broadcloth coat, pulled out a few coins and held them out to me.

"Is this five dollars, sir?"

A quick count told me she had less than a dollar, not even enough for the cheapest rag doll. I patted her on the head and said, "I'm sorry. Maybe Santa will bring her for you on Christmas."

I went back inside, disappointed in myself. I shouldn't have gotten her hopes up about Santa bringing her the doll, but what else could I have said? Every day after that I would see the little tyke standing outside my window, staring at the china doll with those big, brown eyes. I suppose she was hoping to see Santa had bought it for her, which of course he never did.

George Patterson wasn't coming by to purchase it either, and I was beginning to worry. A five-dollar doll was too expensive an item not to sell and Christmas was only two days away. At least the other toys were selling.

I was in the back of the store counting sacks of flour when the jingle of the bell above the front door alerted me to a new customer entering. Wiping my hands on my apron, I went to greet whoever it was. Maybe it would be George Patterson coming for the doll! It wasn't, but I wasn't disappointed either. It was my lovely bride bringing me my lunch.

"Brrrr! That wind sure does cut through a person," Amy said as she stomped the snow off of her shoes.

I took the basket from her and led her to the stove. "Let me get you a chair while you warm yourself. Can't have you catching a cold."

"Oh, Samuel, you worry too much. I'm fine," she smiled.

I placed a quick kiss on her wind-reddened cheek. "I'm not taking any chances. Now, sit and warm yourself."

Rubbing her hands in front of the hot stove, she said, "I don't think I'll ever get used to the winters here. The wind blows constantly and chills you right to the bone. I wonder how that little girl stands it?"

"Little girl?" I asked.

"Yes, the one that's been standing in front of your window every day for a week now. The poor little thing must be half frozen."

The girl had become such a fixture with her daily visits, I had forgotten she was even there. "Well, if she gets cold enough she can always go home. I wonder who she belongs to?"

"She's one of the Baxter Brood," she told me. "At least that's what someone said."

"Baxter Brood?"

"There are ten in all. Their father died last year from an illness. With all the medical bills, the mother had to sell the farm and move into town. From what I hear, she takes in laundry and barely makes enough to keep food on the table. Poor woman."

Before I could respond, the bell tinkled and the little girl came in. She stood quietly next to the door, her hands clasped together in front of her. Amy invited her to come sit with her by the stove. "No, thank you, Ma'am," she replied shyly.

I went over to her and asked, "What can I do for you today?"

"How much for the pretty doll in the window, sir?"

"She's still five dollars."

The disappointed look on her dirty little face nearly broke my heart. Her mother obviously wouldn't be able to buy her that doll, or anything else for that matter, for Christmas. Like most people in town, a proud lot, her mother probably wouldn't accept any charity, but I wanted to do something for this sweet child. I asked her how much money she had. She wiped her runny pug nose on her sleeve, then pulled ninety-five cents from her pocket.

The hopeful look she gave me that somehow her pittance had magically become five dollars was too much. I couldn't sell her the china doll for ninety-five cents, but I could let her have one of the rag dolls. I would be taking a loss, but who cared for that? It was Christmas after all.

Even though she was disappointed not to get the doll she had wanted, she was still happy when she left with the rag doll carefully cradled in her arms. Amy stood up, walked over to me and kissed me. "That was a nice thing you did. If she's anything like me when I was her age, she won't let that doll out of her sight for a minute."

The next day, Christmas Eve, I was still feeling good about my little act of Christmas kindness as I walked the short distance from our rented house to the store. The street was nearly deserted in the brisk early morning, so it wasn't hard to identify the little girl walking toward me.

"Merry Christmas!" I said to her.

"Merry Christmas, sir."

"Where's your dolly? Do you have her under your coat to keep her warm?"

"No, sir. I don't have her anymore."

"You don't?" I asked. That almost made me mad. I went out of my way to be nice to the little tyke and she repaid me by losing the doll after only one day!

"No, sir. I gave her to Betty."

Bewildered, I demanded, "Who is Betty?"

"Betty is my best friend."

"So you gave her the doll? Why? I thought you wanted her?"

"No, sir. The doll was always for Betty. She doesn't have anybody in the whole world. Her family was killed in a fire and I wanted her to have someone to talk to when I'm not with her. Merry Christmas, sir!"

I was stunned and ashamed of myself. All day at the store I kept thinking how this little girl, who had next to nothing to call her own, wanted nothing for herself. Her only thoughts were for her friend. When I sold her the doll at cost, I thought I was being generous to someone less fortunate than me. I was never so wrong.

At five o'clock I began to close up for the day. Amy would have a special dinner ready, but I was still too miserable to enjoy it. I had just flipped the "open" sign to "closed" when George Patterson pounded on the door.

"Glad I caught you Ritter. It's been a very hectic week at the bank and I forgot to come by for that china doll I saw in your window. I see it's still there so I guess I'm not too late."

The thought of one of his privileged brats owning that doll suddenly became repugnant to me. "Sorry, George, but she has been sold. As a matter of fact, I was just going to wrap her up. Is there anything else you might want instead?"

Once I got rid of George, I locked the door and pulled the blinds. Carefully, I wrapped the china doll with the best wrapping paper I sold. Then I remembered Amy saying there were ten in the Baxter Brood. Hurriedly, I wrapped nine more presents and placed them carefully in a sack.

Then I recalled how Amy said Mrs. Baxter could barely keep food on the table, so I threw in a ham, beans, carrots, a couple cans of cranberry sauce and a fist full of candy.

The snow was falling heavily as I walked toward the Baxter house. I had never been there before, but I recalled seeing the sign for her laundry business.

The streets were dark and empty as everyone was snug in their homes enjoying their Christmas Eve dinners. Mine would have to wait. I had this one errand to perform first.

The Baxter home was little more than a rundown shanty, but the laughter and the warm glow shining through the window bespoke a family that had everything they needed—each other.

I didn't want to intrude, or take the risk Mrs. Baxter would refuse my gifts, so I set the sack down in front of the door. I knocked on the door and then ran around the corner so as not to be seen. The door opened and Mrs. Baxter stepped out into the cold night air wrapping a shawl around her thin shoulders. Her children, pushing and shoving each other were right behind her to see who was at their door.

The kids squealed in delight when they saw the presents in the sack. Mrs. Baxter shushed them back inside, took one more look around to see who had left the sack, then dragged it inside. I stood there for a few minutes, trying to rub the cold out of my arms when I heard a child's gleeful shout, "Mommy! It's the china doll I wanted for Betty!"

Then I heard Mrs. Baxter say, "Apparently Santa wanted you to have her, Sara. You promise to take good care of her?"

"Oh, yes, Mommy! I'll take very good care of her. The nice man at the store said Santa might bring her, but how did Santa know?'

I could see Mrs. Baxter looking out the window as she answered. "Santa has his ways and God bless him."

Winter Holidays Acrostic
by Tanja Cilia

Wrapping paper for the gifts;
I sit down and write my lists...
Nuts to nibble, fruit to peel;
Trips to shop for the best deal.
Eggnog, ice-cream, sleigh bells, snow;
Ribbons, parties, pantomime show.
Holiday goodwill, pageant, parade...
Oh what fun's bought with the money paid!
Lights all around, a wonderful show
Icicles, tinsel, angel-hair, snow.
Dressing for cold days, perhaps rain, too
And can we fit in, a trip to the zoo?
Yuletides bring the year to a close
So here's to many more of those!

Place at the Table
by Helen B. Henderson

The smell of turkey permeated the kitchen as Claire peeled potatoes for Thanksgiving dinner. *Finally,* she thought, *this will be my year.* She hummed her favorite carol as she pictured herself in her new black velvet dress sitting at the adult table for the holidays.

The tune stopped mid-note as her mother walked in, phone in hand. Claire knew her mother's look meant bad news. "Please let me move up this year," the fourteen-year-old whispered under her breath.

"Claire, go down to the cellar and bring up some more potatoes. Cousins Mike and Irene from western Pennsylvania decided to spend their anniversary in New York City, so I invited them to Thanksgiving dinner here."

Stifling a moan, Claire managed to ask, "How many, Mom?"

"Four. Mike and Irene, Billy is ten and the baby is eighteen months." Seeing the look on her daughter's face she continued, "I'm sorry, hon. I know you had hoped to sit at the big table, but I need you to help me out and be hostess at the children's table. Maybe next year."

This was my one time to sit with the grown-ups, Claire fumed. *Now I don't know when I'll be able to sit there.* The family had grown so much they could barely crowd enough chairs around the table. She didn't want to wait until she grew old. She didn't want anyone to die, or anything bad to happen. But she really wanted to sit with the adults this year.

31

She had been so hopeful. Her aunt planned to visit an old friend in Texas so there would be an empty spot at the adult's table. It was only for this one time, but as the oldest at the children's table, Claire would move up and sit in the elderly aunt's spot.

Fighting back her disappointment, Claire asked. "Do you want me to take care of the baby?"

"That would be great," came the answer she dreaded. "I know Irene would appreciate the break."

In the bustle of helping prepare dinner for thirty people, Claire didn't have time to dwell on her disappointment. Her mother watched as Claire went about stirring the various pots boiling on the stove and basting the large turkey. Then she smiled as Claire started humming the holiday tunes along with the old black radio on the windowsill.

As the men moved the heavy wooden picnic table into the kitchen, Claire's mood darkened. Her humming stopped.

She loved the summer picnic table. For barbeque get-togethers with friends, it sagged in the middle with roasted corn and watermelon. But Claire hated the winter table used to seat all the "children." To her, the contrast between the detailed carved legs of the family's large oak table and the drab rough planks of the picnic was just another way she didn't fit. She wasn't a child, but not an adult either.

"Mom, how will we fit everyone?" Claire asked as she slid chairs for the adults into place. "There's not enough space."

"Irene is left-handed; place her on the corner," her mother directed. "That will make enough space for Mike to sit next to her. There won't be much elbowroom, but we can just fit everyone. Put the armed chair on the end and with a little shifting, the two long benches will slide under the picnic table with just enough space for the baby chair to fit in the corner."

As guest after guest arrived, Claire kept to herself in the kitchen.

"Wouldn't you like to come out and see everyone?" Claire's mother asked on one of her frequent trips to the kitchen. "I can watch the pots for a few minutes," she offered as she filled another tray with the appetizers she and Claire had made the day before.

"That's okay, Mom. You go be hostess. I'm fine."

Claire's mother gave the teen a big hug and a whispered "thank you" before returning to the growing crowd of relatives.

Although usually large and spacious, the kitchen walls seemed to bow out as the various aunts, uncles, cousins, and grandparents took their places. Chairs shifted, then shifted again as people tried to find an open spot between table legs.

Well trained in her responsibilities as hostess, Claire helped serve dish after dish to the children scrunched on the picnic table benches. With a sigh, she slid into the empty spot on the edge of the bench. There was so little room, even thin as she was, she was kept sliding off.

"Here, little one," Claire offered the baby a spoonful of mashed potatoes, deftly sweeping the spoon out of the small grasping hands. Every few spoonfuls, she handed the baby the bottle of milk and took a forkful from her own plate.

The dinner seemed to last forever. Claire sighed as she watched the horde of relatives retire to other parts of the house. Relishing the solitude, Claire ate the rest of the now-cold food on her plate. Washing the dishes, she listened as laughter and carols drifted into the room. Behind the young girl, her mother stood in the doorway, watching, before returning to her duties as hostess.

ᚦ　ᚦ　ᚦ

The next morning when Claire's mother came downstairs, the fourteen-year-old already had the good china piled on the counter ready to be put back on the high cupboard shelves until the next family event.

"Claire, would you like to go out to dinner tomorrow night with your father and me?"

After a moment Claire looked up from greasy roasting pan she was scrubbing. "Just the three of us?" It had been years since just the three of them had gone out to dinner. The arrival of John, Jim, and Karen had signaled the end of the special times and the beginning of her responsibilities as the oldest.

"Yes, Sandra will watch your brothers and sister. I thought we'd go out to the mall and do some Christmas shopping. Then swing by to pick up your father. If everyone has enough energy, maybe we'll go to the movies after dinner. That new movie you wanted to see came out last week and tomorrow might be our only chance to see it at the theater."

The next morning, her mother ironed an embroidered skirt and jacket for Claire to wear.

"It's the holidays; we might as well dress up a little," came the answer to the teen's quizzical look. Claire was even more surprised when her mother came downstairs in her own ankle-length skirt and knee-high boots.

I'm going to record this in my diary, Claire promised herself in the car riding home from the mall. Over her shoulder, the pile of bags spilled from the back seat to the floor, including one hiding a special purchase her mother wouldn't show her. Claire didn't dare hope that dinner and the movies might still be in her future. She didn't want this special day to end. It had been years since her mother and she had an entire day to themselves.

Claire's misgivings didn't become reality. At home, her father jumped in the car. Instead of his usual denim jeans, he wore a fine sweater and poplin slacks. Before Claire could see what they were, her father slipped three pink slips of paper into his pocket.

"Wow," he exclaimed as he pushed bags out of the way. "Did you guys leave anything at the mall?"

"There's a few things left," mother and daughter chorused.

"I took care of the reservations," Claire's father said.

Reservations? Claire thought. *For dinner? Tickets? Maybe I will get to see that new movie.*

Later that night, pillows stuffed behind her back, Claire looked at her mementos of the day. Carefully she placed the movie ticket stubs and the napkin from the steak house in the back of her diary. Dinner at somewhere other than the local hamburger stand was special itself. She even had a dessert she didn't have to share. It was a fact she noted in her diary along with four stars next to the date.

One refrain kept running through Claire's head as she turned out the light and curled up beneath her soft quilt.

I finally got my place at the table!

Home for the Holidays
by Aubrie Dionne

The irony of stepping off the glorious stage at Carnegie Hall to stumbling up the rickety steps of her mother's covered porch in Boone, North Carolina, mocked Camilla Lee in a cruel twist of fate beyond tears. As she dragged her suitcase up behind her, she wondered how she rose from such a humble upbringing to the New York Philharmonic's principle violinist at the young age of twenty two. It was a musing even her parents gawked at, as if a sweet strawberry sprouted from their wild grape vines.

"My goodness, Camilla Lee," her mom's voice danced in the sweet accent of southern grace. "I was beginning to think that you weren't comin' home for Christmas at all this year."

"I had to finish a holiday concert." Camilla dished out her lame excuse like one would hand a store bought fruit cake over to a disliked neighbor. She stood at the doorstep with her violin strapped to her back and her suitcase leaning against her leg. Her black concert dress hung off her slim frame like a shroud and snow crusted her diamond studded high heels.

"One of these days, you should invite us up to see your concerts," her mom offered. "We could drive on up in the old pickup truck."

Camilla squirmed as if it were a threat. She was thankful that she could blame her shudders on the cold. The thought of her parents mingling with New York's high society and her artsy musician friends made her stomach churn.

Her mother's eyes crinkled with an all-knowing wisdom and compassion. For a moment

Camilla wondered if she saw everything about her all too well. Could she really be that shallow and transparent?

Her mom filled the awkward silence with her love, "My heavens, let's get you inside, out of this cold air."

After a quick embrace, Camilla picked up her suitcase and followed her mother into the warmth of the front hallway. Her room was upstairs on the right, but Camilla didn't want to venture back into the past just yet. She looked into the den and saw Granny just where she left her, dozing by the fireplace with her loose knitting in her lap. The familiar scent of apple pie baking in the kitchen made for sleepy dreams.

"Hey Joe, your little girl's home," her mom called out, her voice almost giddy.

Camilla heard a creak in the floorboards upstairs. Her dad emerged from the bedroom, a civil war history book in his hand. He looked older than she remembered, his hair thin and tinged with gray.

"It's good to have you home," he said, descending the stairs in humble steps to embrace his only daughter. "How's life in the big city?"

Camilla looked down to the book title in his hand, using his passion to lure him away from personal questions, "Reading about Gettysburg again, Dad?" She should have known better than to get him started. For him, the war had never ended.

"If General Hooker hadn't been replaced by Meade, Robert E. Lee would have won that war. It was that third day of battle that got 'em. Pickett's charge. Over twelve thousand confederates fought against the center of the Union line on Cemetery Ridge."

Camilla had heard this tale an uncountable number of times, "General E. Lee, eh?" She was named after him, after all. It was a pity that her parents choose a war hero and not a musical virtuoso.

"He was the greatest General that the South had."

Camilla managed a smile, "Well, I'm going up to my room. I have a lot of practicing to do."

"Why, you only just got here," her mom said from the kitchen as she battled with pots and pans, an army of her own to manage. "Why don't you help me with this pot roast for Christmas dinner tomorrow night?"

Camilla already felt stifled and she'd only been there a total of five minutes, "Nah, I'm too tired from traveling."

"You know Granny's been wantin' to teach you that new knitting pattern-"

"I'll learn it later," Camilla said sternly. After an icy moment of silence, she pushed past her dad to her room. If only it was that easy to escape from her life.

🕯 🕯 🕯

A scratching sound awoke Camilla from her dreams. At first she thought a mouse ran across the old floorboards. She stuck her head up from the homespun quilts. A shadow flickered from her windowpane at the drafty end of her bedroom. It was a dry grating noise, like a fingernail on glass or a dog dragging a bone.

Camilla pulled off her heavy comforter and tiptoed to the window. The branches of an overgrown evergreen blew in the wind, hitting the thin pane. Of course, no one slept in her room while she was gone, and her dad must have forgotten to cut it back. Turning open the crank, Camilla reached out and tried to break the longest branches.

A dark silhouette stood against the trees in her backyard. There were no neighbors for miles, yet someone was waiting, watching her from the woods. Before she could turn to the door to alert her parents, she felt an icy wind blow around her, sweeping her off her feet. Suddenly she was standing in knee deep snow below the window.

Disoriented, Camilla hugged her shoulders and narrowed her eyes against the cold. Her flannel pajamas fluttered, thin as rice paper in the wind gust. Jerking her head around, she located the dark silhouette. With a drop of her jaw, she recognized the man that beckoned her out of her warm bed. His face was illustrated all over her father's books.

She shook her head to try to wake herself, but this dream held fast, unwilling to let her go. Meanwhile, the man adjusted his wool overcoat and bowed in greeting.

Her voice was incredulous, "Robert E. Lee?"

He nodded solemnly, as if her question was normal. "I'm here to talk about the past."

"I already know a whole ton about the civil war," she replied, rolling her eyes and wondering if she'd ever wake up. The forced homecoming must have stirred up memories that were teasing her sanity. If only her dad could have dreamt this dream instead.

Robert E. Lee took a step toward her and looked in her eyes almost in accusation. "Not my past. Yours."

She put a hand on her side and titled her head, "What do you know about me?"

"It is not for me to tell you what I know," he replied, eyebrows raised. "It is up to you to find yourself."

His riddle sat between them unresolved. Camilla could only stand and gape in silence. She had to remind herself that he was a fixture of her overly burdened imagination and that the dream would fizzle out soon enough.

"Come, walk with me," he said, gesturing for her to follow him into the darkness of the woods.

Camilla was about to refuse to follow him anywhere, nevermind the thick forest that lurked in her backyard in the heart of winter, in the crux of night. But when she turned around, her house was gone and frost laden woods surrounded her in all directions. The honorable Robert E. Lee was better company than roaming underneath the shadowy bows alone.

She stepped closer to him and demanded, "Where's my home?"

"Now that's the question," he said, turning back around in her direction. "Dear Camilla, what, exactly, do you consider to be your home?"

Camilla quirked her eyebrows and frowned. Her home was located on Blue Ridge Parkway in Boone, North Carolina. It was the same old house that she was born in, grew up in, and visited when she had a break from college. She'd always thought of it as a kind of prison, a place where her dreams could not possibly grow to be what they should. Now that it was gone, she felt a hole in her heart, like a piece of her soul was stripped away.

Robert E. Lee went on as if she'd given him the right answer, "You see, so many people lose sight of who they are in life, where they came from." He sighed, and the bows of the evergreens trembled, "The Civil War tore apart families, pitting brother against brother. People got so riled up that they forgot what was important, what we were fighting for."

Usually she was bored into a coma-like state by the country's history, but a conviction in his voice drew her in. She found herself trailing his footsteps in the crushed snow. They broke free of the forest and entered a clearing where the moon shone down diaphanous light.

"It was Lincoln that reminded the North and South that we were once knit together, that we must embrace those that we fought so hardly against if we were ever to stand united again."

A thread of thought seemed to pull his sentiments toward her own situation, but she couldn't quite figure it out, like one of those picture puzzles that never came into focus.

"What do you mean?"

"Ah, that's for you to discover on your own," Lee said with a smile that was wise and somber. His body began to glow faintly, as if every particle that made him whole suddenly separated and twinkled in and out of existence.

He spoke again, but the words seemed to come from his mind and not his mouth, "Bear in mind what is important in life." In seconds, he faded into shadow, disappearing against the backdrop of pine needles and woods. It was only then that she remembered that Lee had been a teacher after the war. Like any great teacher, he was only guiding her, allowing her to find her own answers to the questions that rumbled deep inside her heart.

Camilla shivered in the dark woods, feeling more alone than when she played her solo in front of the orchestra. She squeezed her eyes shut, trying to rid herself of this strange dream, but every time she opened them she was in the same dark place.

A shriek erupted in the night behind her, and she whizzed around, breath pluming in sporadic huffs. The bows of the great evergreens swayed as a gigantic flying shadow emerged, swooping over her head. It was a bald eagle, impossibly large with a wing span three times her height and golden eyes that pierced the night sky. It landed in front of her, flapping its wings to steady itself in the snow.

Camilla began to back away, but the bird shrieked again and turned around, displaying its great mottled wings. It was an invitation to ride.

The trees rustled in the wind, as if in anticipation of her decision. Their trunks seemed to press in, long black bodies slanting toward the sky above her head. She had a sudden urge to get out of the branches' reach and the eagle was the fastest way available. Its wings glimmered in the moonlight as she stepped toward it. The ethereal shine looked unsubstantial as a ghost, yet when her fingers brushed the feathers, they felt soft and real to her touch. Camilla lifted herself onto its back. With a flutter of wings, they rose above the woods, riding into the star-spangled sky.

It was unlike anything she'd done before. Coasting a mere breath from the tips of the evergreens, she soared, clinging to the eagle's back. The wind ripped through her hair, taking the elastic with it, and her long braid unraveled to fan out behind her like a cape.

She heard a chorus of carolers sing yuletide favorites below and was touched by the sentiment in their words. Although amateur in technique, the rise and fall of the voices resonated in her heart. Why hadn't she ever gone caroling with her parents? Had she always been too involved with her practicing growing up?

Camilla felt tears in the corners of her eyes, and she knew it wasn't because of the winter wind. Time felt as though it slipped through her fingers. The eagle cawed plaintively over its shoulder as if it could feel her pain. They descended down into the deep woods.

At last, she was home. Camilla jumped off the eagle's back and ran to the front door, desperately wiggling the knob. The metal was rigid and cold as ice in her hand, and the door refused to budge. She rang the buzzer, but no one came to answer. Walking along the side of the house, she could see her parents sitting on the sofa by the fire and Granny rocking in the chair.

Camilla wanted nothing else than to be with them. Why had she been so eager to get away before? Pounding her fists on the window pane, she yelled for her parents. They carried on without her, chuckling at some joke as they watched the fire crackle.

Camilla turned back to the eagle, but it was rising, flying away.

"Wait!" she called. "You can't leave me here."

The air grew chill around her and flurries kissed her cheek. The lights in the house slowly dimmed until all she could see was the white light of the moon. She blinked. A cave stood where her house had been, a golden light flickering like an ember at its core.

Camilla balked. She was not about to go in there. But the wind blew so hard, it pushed her forward as the trees reached out to hold her back. She could not stay in the forest. If Robert E. Lee was from the past and the eagle brought her to the present, she knew her future lurked in that cave.

Camilla walked in slowly, her white, snow-drenched socks making imprints in the mud. The path was clear and the light kept flickering, drawing her in. She heard a dry whistle in the air, an old Dixie tune that pulled at the corners of her memory. The farther she went, the more she could make out the form of a man ambling toward her. In one hand he carried a rusty pick, in the other, an empty cage.

No, not an empty cage, she corrected herself. On the bottom lay the tiny bones of a canary.

The light on his helmet dimmed and his head sagged down to his chest. She thought he'd fall over and contemplated going over to help him stand when the flickering light came back on and he pressed forward in arduous steps.

"Christmas is comin' soon," he said, his eyes glazing over. She couldn't tell if he was talking to her or the wind. "I'll be gettin' out of here to see the family."

"Sir," Camilla replied. "Your bird, it's dead."

The man picked up the cage for her to see, "Good ol' Polly? Why she's fine."

He put the cage down and fell to his knees, hitting the hard earth with the sharp end of his pick.

"Just a few more days and I'll be out."

Camilla stood for long moments, watching him work. "Don't you have some information for me? Something maybe about the future?"

"The future." His eyes squinted. "Naw. Don't know anythin' about the future."

Camilla sighed. Would this dream never end? The miner must be the key. If only she got him talking, then she could find out how to get home again.

"Please, sir."

The rock chipped and a large piece of slate crashed down, sending dust scattering around the cave. Camilla coughed and waved her arms. When she looked up, she saw a hole in the cavern wall. The miner had moved to another spot, allowing her to look through. Taking a deep breath, Camilla peered in.

There was a funeral below. She could make out white lilies and people dressed in black. Her parents were seated in the front row. Her mother's face was obscured by a handkerchief, but her father stared stoically ahead. Camilla looked in further. Granny lay in an oak coffin, which rested on a pedestal. She wore the sweater that she'd been knitting all along.

Camilla's heart fell to her feet. Where was she?

As if in answer to her question, the miner's pick sunk into the earth, and he pulled it out awkwardly, creating another hole. Camilla ran over and looked through, although she already knew what she'd see.

It was Carnegie Hall, and she stood on stage. She was playing Brahm's double concerto, the orchestra swelling behind her in a glorious crescendo of rising thirds. She had skipped the funeral for her concert.

"It's only when the end comes that you realize what's important," the miner whispered. His pick hit the bottom of a large boulder and the rock ceiling crumbled. A stone hit her head and she fell to the floor.

🕯 🕯 🕯

Camilla awoke to the sound of her mother's humming. She opened her eyes and saw bright light.

"Mornin' hun," her mother said. "You've been sleepin' a good part of the day."

Her voice broke on her words, "Where's Granny?"

"Why you know the answer to that question," her mother said. Camilla craned her neck up with worry. She couldn't tell if her mother was being sarcastic or stern.

"Well, don't get yourself up in a tither! She's down in her chair, waitin' to teach you some knittin'."

Camilla eased back in relief and rubbed the back of her head. There was a large welt that was sore when she touched it.

"February 26," she said, still groggy from sleep.

"What's that, dear?" Her mother was busy tying the drapes up, letting more light in.

"It's my next concert," Camilla replied, her tone determined. "I want you and dad to come."

Holiday Romances

Ginny's Gift
by Jamie Hill

"Merry Christmas to you, too." Ginny Reese shoved the thirty-nine cent tip in her uniform pocket and tried to hang on to her holiday spirit. The change jingled and she stopped clearing dishes long enough to glance in her pocket. Quick mental math confirmed she'd made less than ten dollars in tips this shift. *Add that to the fifty-six bucks I've been saving, and I still don't have enough for the video game player Shaun wants.*

She sighed and returned to bussing the table. With only five days until Christmas, it was going to be slim pickings under the tree. Her eight-year-old son had always been easy to please, but this year, he'd set his sights on a hand-held game system all the other kids seemed to have. It was the only gift Shaun talked about.

She'd found a nice used one at a pawn shop for a hundred dollars, quite a bargain over department store prices. The manager promised to hold the system for her, but only until the 23. Time was running out. At this rate, she wouldn't have the full hundred until February.

"Oh, Miss? May I have my ticket, please?" A customer from a nearby table waved.

"I'll be right with you." Ginny gave the older couple an apologetic smile. She swabbed the table she'd just cleared and hefted the bussing tub of dirty dishes behind the counter. As she tallied up the diners' tab, she saw the owner watching her from the kitchen. Ray didn't look happy. Since his wife had taken ill, he rarely looked happy anymore. Ginny hoped that the overburdened man could keep the café open and she'd still have a job after the holidays.

As she passed by the front windows, she stopped and glanced outside. Another gloomy, overcast day. Cold weather had hit Chicago in October and hadn't released its grasp since. Flowers were dead, and the grass had all turned brown. Everything looked bleak and dreary.

A lock of her wavy, red hair had come loose from her ponytail and Ginny shoved it behind her ear. Turning away from the window, she sighed. *How did I wind up in Chicago, and what am I still doing here?*

She took care of her last customers and pocketed another dollar tip. "What's with people?" she muttered after the seniors had gone. "It's almost Christmas, for crying out loud. Where's the spirit and generosity everyone talks about?"

"Probably in the tank, along with the economy," someone replied over her shoulder. Ginny spun around, her face burning with embarrassment.

The new customer had apparently just slipped in, and she'd been so caught up in her own thoughts she hadn't noticed. Her face grew even warmer when she realized the man was several inches taller than her and extremely handsome. Wavy brown hair touched his collar and matched the deep chocolate color of his eyes. "I'm so sorry," she whispered. "I should never have said that."

He waved her apology off. "Forget it. A dollar isn't nearly a good enough tip for a waitress of your caliber."

Ginny narrowed her eyes. "How do you know what kind of a waitress I am? Maybe I dumped soup in his lap and served her a burnt pork chop."

"I highly doubt that." He lowered his voice confidentially. "But you're right. I was judging the book by its cover." The man glanced up and down her body and gave a low whistle. "But, what a gorgeous cover it is!"

She couldn't help but smile. "Now you're blowing smoke up my hooie. All right, mister, find yourself a seat. Menu's on the table."

His eyes sparkled, accenting a charming grin. "Yes, Ma'am. Sit anywhere?"

Ginny waved a hand around the nearly empty café. "Take your pick. Knock yourself out."

He grabbed a chair and took a seat. "All right, all right. Just wanted to make sure you'd be my waitress, is all."

She smiled. *I'm not falling for his lines, but I guess it won't hurt to humor him a little bit.* "Seeing as I'm the only waitress here today, chances are good."

"Whew," he swiped at his brow, feigning relief, and picked up the menu. "What do you recommend?"

"George's Sub Shop down the street."

He blinked, surprise evident on his face.

Ginny laughed. "Just kidding. Ray makes the best hamburgers around. You can't go wrong with any of them. If you're in the mood for something more, the meatloaf is good today."

"No, a burger is fine. I'll take the deluxe with fries and a strawberry shake."

She glanced over his trim physique, wondering how he ate like that and stayed in such good shape.

He must have spotted her once-over, because he smiled. "Yes? Something you'd like to ask me?"

"No!" Ginny's face heated and she was sure it was bright red this time. "I just, uh, could never eat like that. And I should *not* have said that. Never mind. I'll put in your order. It usually doesn't take long."

Before she could scamper off, he chuckled. "You have an open invitation to say anything you like with me." He acted like he was checking out her backside, and then shook his head. "Whatever your diet regimen is, keep it up. I've never seen a better looking hooie."

"Hey," she snapped, teasingly. "Enough of that."

He held up his hands innocently. "It was your word. I just thought it was cute, is all. Almost as cute as you…" He squinted to read her nametag.

"Ginny," she offered, trying not to be bowled over by his lavish compliments. In her twenty-nine years, she'd figured out that most men were the same. They usually had one thing in mind. The "hungry wolf" look in this fellow's face bore her theory out.

"Pleased to meet you, Ginny." His expression softened into that killer smile she'd glimpsed earlier. "I'm Mark, by the way. Mark Tanner."

She looked at the floor quickly. "Your, uh, lunch should be here soon." Ginny hurried away from his table, leaving the timbre of his soft laughter behind her.

She clipped the order ticket on the spinning rack between the counter and the kitchen.

Ray grabbed the ticket and looked at her questioningly. "Problem?"

"No," she insisted. "Not at all. Thanks." She turned away, hoping her face wasn't still flushed. She felt stupid letting the forward customer get to her. He was just flirting. *Just being a man.* She'd bolster her defenses and wouldn't let him get to her when she returned to his table.

Easier said than done. The man liked to talk. Even after she delivered his food and walked away, he spoke across the restaurant to her. He chatted about his day, the metro traffic, and cold weather. He'd occasionally toss in a comment about how pretty she was. Ginny did her best to keep working and ignore him.

If he weren't so darned handsome! She wished for more customers to come in and give her something to do. The noon rush was over and the place was like a morgue. She filled salt and pepper shakers, and listened to the chatty hunk talk.

"So, you ready for Christmas?" Mark asked shoving his plate away.

Resigned to his questions, Ginny sighed. "No. I could use a little more shopping time." *And money to shop with.* "We don't even have our tree, yet. My son's really on me about that."

"How old's your son?" His eyes crinkled when he smiled.

Thinking about the sandy-haired cutie brought a smile to Ginny's face, too. "He's eight...going on sixteen. Has an answer for everything and enough charm to get away with it." Gazing at the expression on her customer's face, she realized she was likely describing Mark, too. "You probably know all about that."

He laughed. "Maybe. Don't have any kids, though. Wish I did. Does his father help keep the boy in line?"

Ginny folded her arms across her chest. *Is he fishing for information?* She'd feed him just a bit. "His *father* dragged us from a nice small town in Kansas to this God-forsaken place with the promise of a new job and a new life. When the job fell through, he rode the first cocktail waitress out of town, in search of the next big prospect."

Mark frowned. "That sucks. So why did you stay? Don't you have family back in Kansas?"

She nodded. "He also left us with nine months to go on a year's lease. Shaun really likes his school, so I thought I'd tough it out." She expelled a breath that made her bangs flutter. "I guess it's just harder this time of year. Plus, the older Shaun gets, the more expensive his toys become."

"That, I know about." Mark nodded. "What did the kid ask Santa for this year?"

Ginny shook her head. "A video game player that's all the rage right now. The Hand-held Z System, I think it's called. If he doesn't get it, the Earth might as well open up and swallow him."

Mark chuckled. "So, is he getting it?"

She raised her eyebrows. "Depends how big of a tip you leave."

His eyes clouded as he apparently registered her meaning. "I'm sorry, Ginny." When he spoke so sincerely, his playboy persona melted away.

She thought, for a moment, she might melt into him.

Ray tapped his fingers on the counter, disturbing the trance-like state she'd fallen into. "Ginny, a moment, please?"

"Be right there," she called, and smiled at Mark. "Guess I need to get busy."

"Understood." He patted his chest pocket and a strange expression crossed his face. He stood and patted all his pockets. "Well, crap."

"What's wrong?"

"I don't seem to have my wallet." He emptied his pockets searching, and finally looked at her with a mortified expression. "I can't believe I did this. I feel so stupid."

"It's not that big of a problem." Ginny calculated the price of his meal in her head. *Right about ten bucks.* She glanced at the owner, then back to Mark. "Not for me, anyway. Ray's been hit by a few dine-and-dashers though, and I'm afraid he takes them pretty seriously. He'll want me to call the cops."

"I'm not a dine-and-dasher!" Mark insisted. "Honestly, I never—"

"Keep your voice down," Ginny responded, digging in her tip pocket. "Look, I believe you. Let me help you out with this, and Ray will never know. It won't be a big deal."

"Oh, no." Mark grimaced as she emptied her pocket onto the table.

She waved him off. "This should cover it. Don't worry about it. Catch me next time." She scooped the money back up and headed toward the counter.

"Ginny, really, I—"

"Nice talking to you." She didn't turn around, just kept walking and talking. "Merry Christmas."

"Yeah, Merry Christmas," he repeated without much enthusiasm.

She heard the tinkle of the bell on the door, and looked up in time to see him walk out. Her heart fell with a thud into her stomach.

What did you expect? she berated herself as she ran his order into the cash register. *You told him not to worry about it.* But she hadn't expected him to agree so easily and leave. Just as she'd started thinking he might be different than all the rest, he went and proved her wrong. He was a man like any other, plain and simple. Take whatever he can get, and go. Thoughts of her ex-husband flooded her mind and she hurried to wipe her eyes before meeting Ray in the kitchen.

                          ô   ô   ô

December twenty-third dawned as gloomily as each day had done for the previous week. Ginny stopped by the pawn shop before her shift at the café and confirmed that the manager had sold the game system to another customer. Now it was time for damage control. She'd have to come up with alternate gifts for Shaun with the sixty-five dollars she'd managed to squeeze out of her meager budget.

Ray was in an unusually cheerful mood when she arrived at work. "Donna's feeling much better! The doctor says she can come home for Christmas."

"Oh, Ray, I'm so glad." Ginny hugged the older man gently. "I know all your family will be there. That's just great."

"I'm as happy as a pig in mud." His wide grin said the same. "I want you to accept this, call it a little Christmas bonus, and buy yourself something." He tucked some cash into her hand.

Ginny looked at the forty dollars with amazement. It hadn't come soon enough to save the video game, but it did mean Shaun could have a decent Christmas. Starting with a tree, which they'd go get that evening. "Thank you so much!" She hugged Ray again, truly grateful for the gift.

The lunch crowd filtered in, and by the time everyone had come and gone, Ginny had another twenty in tips. She chuckled at the irony, while her mind whizzed, deciding what kinds of gifts she could buy for Shaun.

The door opened and she looked up to greet the incoming customer. Ginny blinked with surprise when she saw Mark standing there, a wrapped present in his hands. "Hey," she murmured.

"Hi." He took a step closer to her. "I feel really bad about what happened the other day."

"I told you, it was no big deal," she insisted.

"But we both know it was." He stared into her eyes. "I came in to try and make it up to you."

She tore her gaze away long enough to look at the present. "You didn't have to."

"I know I didn't." Mark reached in his pocket and pulled out a twenty dollar bill. "I had to do this—pay for my tab, and your tip."

"Oh, thanks." Ginny took the cash, surprised.

"But this is just a little something I thought you could use." He held out the gift. "Did I tell you I work for KMNO Radio Chicago?"

"No." Confused, Ginny shook her head as she accepted the package. "What does that have to do with—?"

He smiled. "We get all kinds of promotional stuff for giveaways. Did you hear your name on the radio this morning? You won a Hand-held Z System video game."

"You're joking!" Ginny's eyes bulged.

"I'm totally serious." He leaned in and spoke softly. "You had a little help with the winning part, but nobody needs to know that or I could lose my job."

"Oh, Mark." Ginny was speechless.

"It was worth it, to see the look on your face right now. I don't get the opportunity to play Santa's helper very often. I had to do it. Truthfully, I just had to see you again."

"Oh, Mark." She was still speechless, but thoughts were forming in her mind.

Happy thoughts.

Ginny threw her arms around his neck and hugged the stuffing out of him. "How can I ever thank you?" She stepped back and, smiling, placed one hand on his chest. "Wait, don't answer that."

"Oh! Please let me answer! Please!" He swept her into his arms.

Happiness overtook her and Ginny closed her eyes for a soft, romantic kiss. When she opened them again, the look she saw reflected in his eyes sent a shiver down her spine. She cleared her throat and stepped back, hugging the box to her chest. "Um, thank you. Seriously. You don't know how much this means."

"I'd like to." He touched her hand. "I'd like to know everything about you, and tell you anything you want to hear about me. I realize that'll take some time, and I'll be patient. Just say I can spend a little bit of Christmas with you. That would mean so much to me."

And to me. Ginny knew they'd have to take things slow, especially with Shaun involved. It'd been a long time since she'd been "courted," and it sounded wonderful to her. She smiled. "How do you feel about picking out a Christmas tree?"

"Sounds like a great place to start."

Ray stepped out of the kitchen, walked past them to the front window and looked out. "Well, what do you know? It's snowing. Doesn't that look pretty?"

She glanced out and spotted big, fluffy flakes covering the ground. "It's beautiful!"

"Very beautiful," Mark added, smiling. He pulled her into his arms and planted a soft kiss on her temple.

Ginny inhaled his masculine fragrance, and reveled in the feel of his strong arms wrapped around her. She nestled her face against his shoulder. *Finally, the holidays are looking up.*

"Merry Christmas," Mark murmured.

She sighed with pleasure. "Yeah. I think it's going to be."

Christmas Bits
by Michael Mohr

Jesus   chaos   peace   poverty   depression
   Order   sanity   security   greed   Jesus
    Giving   Joy   lost jobs
Insecurity   murder   elation   Jesus
Homelessness Santa Claus   parties midnight church
   Shopping   volunteering   cold   snow   Jesus

What are we to make of the chaos of life
       in our time   this Christmas?
Reality seems to be the antithesis of the ideal.
God seems either asleep or impotent.
Can we survive the frenetic pace of life and the
holiday?

Even in the chaos there is order.
"His name shall be called 'Emmanuel' which
means
      GOD WITH US"
Jesus so pervades the chaos that—
      Yes we will survive!

59

My Christmas Luck
by Nicole Zoltack

Pauline Gregson rubbed her hands together. The resulting friction did little to warm her as she waited for the bus. Public transportation was not her idea of a good time, but her car had broken down the week before and the mechanic was backed up. The chances of her being able to use her car before Christmas seemed unlikely at this point.

The street was well lit but deserted, and Pauline checked her watch again. The bus was running late. On the coldest day of the year so far. *Just my luck.*

A car pulled up alongside her, and the window rolled down. "Need a lift?"

Pauline didn't step up to the window but eyed the man with open curiosity. With sandy brown hair and twinkling eyes, he hardly seemed the type to kidnap and harm her. But you could never be too sure.

"I'm waiting for the bus."

"It's gonna be a long wait," he warned. "Just heard on the radio that there's a major traffic jam that way." He pointed in the direction the bus would be coming from. "Multi-car pile up, if I'm not mistaken."

Pauline groaned. At this point, she might as well walk home. The dreadful night and freezing wind would not make for a pleasant journey.

As she debated her options, the man said, "I know how this must appear, me offering you a lift. But I just thought I would ask. At least let me buy you a cup of coffee." He nodded toward the coffee shop behind her. "Warm you up. Then you can decide if I'm harmless or not." The man grinned broadly, and two large dimples appeared, giving him a boyish charm.

Pauline smiled despite herself. "Make it a hot cocoa and you got a deal."

"Great."

Pauline headed toward the shop's door while the man parked. She opened the door for them, belatedly noticing his outstretched arm.

The harried waitress told them to claim any table, and Pauline followed the man. Tall, with broad shoulders, but slim, he was pleasing to the eye.

Pauline had a habit of distrusting men, especially good-looking ones. She had been burned too many times in the past to fall for someone on looks alone.

The man ordered a black coffee for himself and her drink. After the waitress left, he held out his hand. "I'm Walter, by the way."

"Pauline." His handshake was firm and, more importantly, warm.

Pauline almost forgot to pull away. "So what brings you into the city on this cold, bitter night?"

Walter laughed, a nice, booming sound. "I was just about to ask you that. My niece loves the city. And she collects pins so I bought her this." He reached into his pocket and pulled out a large, glittery "I heart New York" pin.

"That's beautiful."

He nodded and tucked it away. "Your turn."

"Coming home from work. My car's in the shop. I don't live in the city so I have to transfer and take a lot of buses."

"Why not the subway?"

61

Pauline shuddered. "I hate the subway. It's dark and crowded and…"

Walter laughed again. "I don't blame you. Never did like the subway myself."

The waitress handed them their drinks. "Anything else?" she asked, cracking her gum loudly.

Walter looked at Pauline, who shook her head, and the waitress turned away.

"If you change your mind and want a dessert," he offered.

She smiled. Try as she might, she was having a hard time not liking the good-looking man sitting across from her. But the weight was finally starting to come off and she wasn't about to blow her diet for a slice of warm apple pie. Although apples were healthy… "What are you doing for the holidays? Going to visit your niece?"

"I wish. No, my Christmas will be a lonely one this year, I'm afraid. My brother and his family are heading down to Florida to visit our parents. Normally I would go, too, but I need to work the next day. Bright and early." He grimaced.

"What do you do?" she asked.

"I'm a consultant for a law firm."

"Sounds like…fun."

Walter winked. "Not always, I'll be honest. But it can be rewarding work."

Pauline lifted an eyebrow.

"At times! Not all lawyers are crooks." He blew onto his steaming black drink before swallowing several gulps.

Pauline's fingers had finally thawed by holding her ceramic mug, and she drank. The sweet bitterness of the liquid chocolate warmed her insides.

"And your holiday plans?" he asked.

Pauline sighed. "None. No family close enough to visit. At least, not with my car out of commission."

"Oh, I'm so sorry." He leaned forward. "So no boyfriend either?"

She offered a wan smile. "I'm between disappointments."

He laughed. "You're too young to be so cynical about love!"

"And you? Do you have someone special in your life?"

For the first time, Walter's face changed from happy-go-lucky to something deeper. "No, no one. My brother says I'm too picky. And maybe I am."

"Well, what do you want in a woman?"

"Someone I can be myself with. Laugh with. Enjoy their company. I'll be honest, I do want someone nice to look at."

"Only nice?" she teased.

He shrugged sheepishly. "She has to be tolerant of my sport obsessions."

"Which teams?"

"Yankees and Giants, mostly."

"I like the Yankees, but I actually didn't grow up around here. I'm from Pennsylvania. So I'm an Eagles fan."

"Ugh." Walter waved her away. "That's it; you pay for your hot chocolate."

She giggled.

"Besides, I don't think I could be with someone who doesn't like coffee."

Pauline blushed. "Your brother's right; you're too picky."

They were quiet for a few moments to finish their drinks. Walt broke the silence first. "So what brings a Pennsylvanian to the Big Apple?"

"My job. I'm a literary agent."

"Oh, wow, now that's an intriguing job. No wonder you think mine so dry and boring."

She giggled. "I never said boring."

"No, but you insinuated it." He turned and stared out the window. Snowflakes began to lightly dust the road. "You still want to wait for the bus?"

During the early part of their conversation, Pauline had constantly glanced outside, waiting to see the bus. But Walter had drawn her from her thoughts of her small apartment, and she had stopped looking until now. The idea of waiting in that bitter cold was even less appealing now. Walking was out of the question, unless it was to the subway. Obviously the buses weren't running along this route tonight.

"I guess not. Can't really say I trust you, being a Giants fan and all that." She winked at him. "But if you're still offering a ride, I'll take you up on it."

Walter smiled. "Good." He waved the waitress over and paid their bill. Pauline tried to hand him some money but he ignored her, gently grabbed her elbow and steered her toward his car. "Where do you live?"

Pauline gave him the address and soon their conversation was reduced to turn left here, right at the light.

She glanced at his side profile. With a slightly too large nose and chiseled jaw, he was nothing like Bill. Or Jake. She couldn't remember a time when she had just relaxed with either of her old boyfriends. They had been too busy trying to impress her, to be something they weren't. Walter was a refreshing change, honest. Disappointment filled her when he pulled in front of her apartment complex. She didn't want Walter to leave just yet.

"Thank you for the ride." She turned in her seat to smile at him, still wearing her seat belt.

"Thank you for the coffee break."

Pauline shook her head. "I should be the one thanking you."

"I never would have stopped for it if you weren't waiting for that bus."

"In that case, you're welcome." She slowly moved her hand to her seat belt.

"Do you want me to walk you to the front door?"

"You don't have to."

Walter shook his head. "Women. Want to be independent but then cry that chivalry's dead. I offered."

Pauline laughed. "I just don't want to further inconvenience you."

"You aren't inconveniencing me. In fact, I have no reason to hurry home. It's lonely and needs to be cleaned and vacuumed…." He shifted the car into drive and turned into a parking spot, leaving the engine running for the heat.

"I'm glad you stopped."

"Me too. Would have been awful to wake up tomorrow morning and read about the poor woman who got frostbite when the buses stopped running."

She shook her head and laughed. "That would make for an awful story."

"I'm not a writer, but this night could have a happy ending."

Pauline's heart began to race. "How so?"

"If you let me see you again. Sometime. For dinner instead of just warm drinks."

His warm, brown eyes looked so hopeful, and Pauline melted. "Yes."

Maybe my luck is finally beginning to change. For once in her life, she dared to believe that her love life might have a happy ending.

Celebrating with Emmanuel
by Michael Mohr

What shall we do about this Christmas this year?
I don't feel much like celebrating.
 My grief is too fresh;
 My wound is unhealed;
 My loneliness is too real.
 Jingle bells and Santa Claus seem too empty
for me.

And yet life goes on. And so must I.
Inescapably Christmas bids me celebrate.
Its joy and life are all around me.
But how can I be merry? How can I celebrate?

I hear beside me the voice of a stranger that I
know intimately.
I am Emmanuel, it says, I can help.
The one you miss lives with me.
Celebrate with me and you celebrate with them.
Sing with me and you sing with them.
Love with me and you will know their love.
Because I Am they are also.

Let's celebrate Christmas together, all of us.

Perceptions on New Year's Eve
by Sandy Lender

Janet narrowed her baby blues at Melissa and lowered a metallic silver streamer from the hanging cabinet above her. Considering they worked with multiple colors of streamers and all sorts of baking products, the wood-paneled kitchen with its dark granite countertops was remarkably tidy. Melissa was nothing if not efficient. At the moment, Miss Efficiency tried to avoid her friend's calculating glare. No one would mistake Janet's scowl for less than measured.

"Wait," Janet growled. "Robert Milton? *The* Robert Milton?"

Melissa tried not to giggle. Failing, she put an over-manicured hand to her mouth. From behind the too-red nails, she said, "Don't act like that. He's loaded."

"Loaded? Mel, he came to the office Christmas party dressed as an elf." She paused as if Melissa needed the moment to recall the image. "A Christmas elf. One of Santa's little helpers. Not even scads of money can make an elf sexy."

Melissa gave way to the giggles then, unwisely turning her back on Janet. She donned a pair of reindeer oven mitts while answering. "It really depends on how you wear the costume."

"No. No, it doesn't. I've never seen a sexy elf and never will."

"Stop right there, liar." She spoke to Janet, but waved her antlered mitts to disperse the heat from the now-open oven. "You're telling me you didn't get all hot and bothered over Orlando Bloom in the hobbit movies?"

"Different kind of elf," Janet muttered, returning to her decorating duties. She taped the silver streamer's end to the cabinet above her head with more gusto than necessary. "Orlando's cuter as a pirate, which, by the way, I don't think Robert could pull off. His hair's too gray."

"You've got your own touches of gray in that mass of brown sugar, girlfriend," Melissa snarked.

"Thanks."

"What?" Melissa acted innocent. "It's charming. It says you have experience and intelligence. It says you can decide decisively whether Orlando Bloom is sexier as an elf or a pirate."

Janet snorted at that. "And I can decide that Robert's glasses are too thick to be either." As if the comment had come out too catty, Janet whirled back to her original complaint. "I can't believe you set me up with Robert Milton, office clown, for New Year's Eve. The one night out of the year that I have to spend at least three hours chained to my blind date's side, whether I like him or not, because of the midnight deadline, and you pick Robert. It's like a bad movie."

"It's not like a bad movie. He has a great sense of humor."

"That's like a guy telling his buddy a girl has a great personality," Janet moaned. "I dread the midnight kiss."

"It's the truth, though! Remember that holiday memo he sent around?"

Janet pursed her lips.

"You thought that was funny," Melissa reminded her. "And you thought it was funny when he gave Old Man Crast a pink tie for a Christmas present."

Janet rolled her eyes heavenward. "That doesn't mean I want to kiss the prankster at midnight." As if a new thought just occurred to her, Janet said, "Tell me Crast isn't invited to this shindig."

"I had to invite him. He's our boss."

"A date with the office clown *and* the boss performing in the karaoke room. I've half a mind to go home right now."

"Oh no you don't!" Melissa barked, dropping a pan of brownie-looking cookies on top of the stove. She pointed an antlered paw at her friend in mock anger. "I'm not serving my world-famous rum balls alone. You get credit for the content of these babies."

"The content. Honey, the alcohol bakes out of them and you know it. Between fake rum balls and non-spiked eggnog, this party is going to be as mild as—"

"Hey, can I help it that half our co-workers are recovering alcoholics?"

Janet smirked. "You're such a goodie two shoes. We work in the wrong business. Our co-workers can't drink and they show up to parties dressed like elves."

"Our co-workers are just trying to have fun. You should join in."

Janet sighed. "I'm trying. Give me more streamers."

"Is that what you're wearing then? You didn't bring a change of clothes?"

Janet glanced down at her jeans and sweater ensemble. "There's nothing wrong with this."

"If we were going on a hay ride for New Year's Eve, there'd be nothing wrong with that.

But we're not. We're hanging out in my fab condo with Dick Clark in one room, a karaoke machine in another, and candlelight in another. You're underdressed no matter which room you step into. I demand you at least let me loan you something dressier. And let me do your nails."

Janet growled.

"No arguing. Just because that weirdo you were engaged to liked your nails long and pretty doesn't mean you have to stop wearing them long and pretty now. There were *some* things he liked that weren't insane."

"Wearing my nails long is a bother when I'm typing," Janet said, miming typing action.

"Wearing your nails long doesn't have to be a reminder of Tomas. It can be a rebellion against his memory. A Gloria Gaynor kind of thing. I will survive. I will wear my nails the way I want to. I'll throw out the bulky sweater and put on my friend Melissa's pretty, flirty top for New Year's Eve."

Janet had to smile at that.

Melissa grinned back. "Right? These fake rum balls have to cool. Let's go find something realistic for you to wear."

"Realistic to wear for my date with an elf."

§ § §

"Wow, Janet," Charlotte Makon said when she appeared in the open doorway. "I hardly recognized you."

Janet unclenched her jaw long enough to say, "Happy New Year, guys," to Charlotte and her date. She gestured them into Melissa's home and closed the door against cold air. "Can I take your coats?"

71

"Sure, thanks. I love what you've done with your hair tonight. I haven't seen it up like that since you were dating Tomas. Don't you think her hair is gorgeous, Bill?"

The man at Charlotte's side said something polite, smiled politely, and politely handed his coat over with Charlotte's. Janet appreciated his tact. She made a quick exit to Melissa's bedroom to deposit the coats and breathe alone for a minute.

Coats already heaped on top of the bed promised her date would stand her up, which pleased her on one level. Even if Robert Milton was a lousy date, it seemed a shame he felt the same about her. She frowned at Charlotte's fake fur as she tossed it on the pile.

She hadn't planned to stand in the room for minutes on end, listening to the sounds of music and laughter from the other rooms in the condominium, so she hadn't turned on the light. In the soft glow of a streetlight streaming through the thin curtains, she stared at the pile of coats, wondering how many of them were recently opened Christmas presents.

"Cripes," she said to herself. Mimicking Charlotte's voice, she screwed up her face and said, "Wow, Janet, you look so nice this evening after letting yourself go for the past six months." She flopped her hand with an aristocratic air as she mewled to herself, "I'm so surprised to see you with makeup after how plain you've been the past six months. I'm stunned to see you haven't flung yourself from the roof at work during the past six months."

"Excuse me," a man interrupted.

She spun in alarm to face the door. The light from the hall cast the man in shadow, thus his muscled silhouette greeted her instead of some look of concern. She was thankful. The last thing she wanted was a pity party with a stranger.

"Didn't mean to startle you," he apologized. "Coat room?"

"Ah, yeah, coats. Here, I can take that for you." She walked toward him, arm outstretched for his jacket. She couldn't see his features yet, and didn't realize he could see hers. Hopefully he didn't notice her checking out his sculpted arms and shoulders in the light from the hall.

"Janet!" The happiness in his tone surprised her.

She stopped abruptly. "Yes?"

"I didn't realize I'd run into you so soon, but, I guess Mel's apartment isn't too big, is it? Robert Milton. We barely know each other."

She hoped he couldn't read disappointment on her face. Plastering her best "that's so nice" smile on, she accepted his jacket. "Pleasure. Yeah, we, uh, work in neighboring departments, I guess you could say."

"Same fussy boss," he joked.

She forced her smile to become a touch more real. *Office clown,* she thought. *Great.* "Yeah, Crast can be a little overbearing, can't he?" she offered.

He swiped his palms across his thighs. "Uh, yeah. Do you mind if I sit down for a minute? I'm not…I mean, I don't want you to think I'm lame or anything, but I'm not one for jumping right into the social mix at parties, if you know what I mean."

"Oh." That was odd. "Oh, sure. Umm. There are a ton of coats in here…"

"That's okay. I don't mean to impose. Sitting next to some clothes won't bother me."

73

Janet walked him over to the bed and the two sat on opposite sides of a huge mound of materials. She couldn't think of anything more bizarre, and found herself still holding his jacket.

"I hope you don't think I'm a complete loser," he said across the dimly lit space.

"We're forty-something. I don't think 'complete loser' is in our vernacular anymore."

He chuckled. "I don't know. I've got a teenage daughter with me for the holidays who accused me of that very thing after the office Christmas party the other week. I don't think I'll ever live down the things she said to me."

"Really? Teens can be cruel. They call it like they see it." As soon as the words left her mouth, Janet felt ashamed for saying them. What right did she have to pass judgment on an age group she had no contact with? What right did she have defending them in front of a man who'd been stung by one?

"That they do," he said. He spoke as if he had something else on his mind. She thought he might want to change the subject, and she hoped he hadn't heard her soliloquy before he'd come into the coat room. "That they do," he continued. "She really ripped into me for my costume."

Janet almost laughed, and thanked her lucky stars the room was dark enough to hide her struggling smile. "You were an elf, weren't you?"

He chuckled. "Yes. And if my daughter's right, I'll lose my job, my reputation as a man, and all ability to comment on sports programs until the Cubs win the World Series."

Now she did laugh. "You're doomed."

"Apparently. But she gave me some good advice."

"After all that negativity, I'd hope."

"She suggested a few improvements."

There was a pause while they listened to the merry-making in the karaoke room.

"I think I hear Crast's voice," Janet finally whispered. While she wanted to ask what improvements the teen had suggested, she didn't think it was any of her business. She was dating the office clown for one evening. A few hours. At the stroke of midnight, she'd find a way to be nowhere near him so she didn't have to kiss him, and she'd make a quick exit home. Tour of duty over.

She looked at him in the dim light. Not sure why…she couldn't see his face.

"You think he's going to sing?" he asked.

"I dread it."

"Ditto. But I have video on my camera. We could capture it for evidence in the future. It could be what saves my job next week."

"You're suggesting blackmail," Janet giggled. So the office clown *did* have a good sense of humor.

"That's exactly what I'm suggesting. Are you in?"

"I'm in." She set his jacket on the bed behind her.

He reached over the pile of coats to offer her his hand, which she didn't find odd until he guided her into the light of the hall. She didn't need a man to steer her around Melissa's condo, but Robert led her as if they were on a covert operation. Something about it made her smile. She glanced from the opening of the great room to Robert's face to say something, and the thoughts in her mind fled.

Covert ops? Crast's choice of song? What had she been about to say?

Robert looked back at her with a twinkle of mischief in his deep blue eyes and a finger pressed to his lips to shush her. As if anyone paid attention to them sneaking up to the back of the crowd. He released her hand, apparently not noticing her staring in slack-jawed amazement at the pillar of manliness before her. He pulled a slim camera from his Docker's pocket and fidgeted with the buttons for a moment. All she could do was watch as a lock of perfect brown hair fell forward while he worked.

What had happened to his coke-bottle glasses? Where was the greasy gray hair that bothered her in the hallways at work? When did he learn that a dark blue button-down VanHeusen set off the color of his face like a Greek Adonis? She struggled for a moment to breathe.

"Robert!" someone shouted. "You're next!"

She saw him object. She saw someone pull on his arm. He handed her the camera. Life moved in some sort of heavy fluid. Sound, cinnamon scent, holly and berry colors, and jovial voices all smeared together in her mind as she watched this handsome man approach the mini stage in Melissa's great room. Melissa tugged on her arm.

"Hey, you. What's got you lookin' like a reindeer caught in the headlights?"

Janet mumbled some sort of response that set Melissa to giggling. "Figured. You know, he told me he was really looking forward to getting to know you better."

Janet shook her head a bit to clear the holiday fog from it. "What's that?"

"Yeah. You look smitten, my dear. I said, he was really looking forward to this evening. Aren't you surprised?"

Janet wasn't sure if it was surprise or shock. "I have to admit…"

Melissa giggled some more. "Yeah, I'll take that as a 'thank you.'"

"I don't understand."

"What's to understand? The guy's handsome, funny, smart, financially secure. Your entire system is attracted to him."

Janet looked to Melissa in almost despair. "But just a couple hours ago I was sure he was a nerd. I was sure I had no interest. What's changed?"

Melissa shrugged. "You took a good look at him?"

"Surely it's more than that. I can't be that shallow."

"Probably. Did you talk to him?"

"Well, yeah, but…" Janet looked back toward Robert with his easy smile on the other side of the great room. From across the crowd, he winked at her and saluted with the microphone. The jazzy piano notes of Harry Connick Jr.'s version of *What Are You Doing New Year's Eve* drifted into the mix of voices and laughter, quieting the buzz a bit.

"I guess I just never listened to him before."

"You never listened to him," Melissa agreed. "You never looked at him. You never paid attention. There's magic at the holidays, whether it's Solstice Night, Christmas Eve, Christmas Day, New Year's Eve, or whatever. It makes people sit up and take note of the bits and pieces they'd otherwise miss. You, Miss Janet, have just fallen for a sexy elf."

Janet shot Melissa an annoyed glance, but her attention drifted back to Robert easily as he began the lyric, "Maybe it's much too early in the game."

Janet gasped, as did half the audience. No one could believe Robert's deep voice mimicked Harry Connick Jr. so perfectly. Melissa laughed lightly and leaned in to whisper in Janet's ear. "Bet you can't wait for midnight now."

Something in the Lights
by Anna Dane

When night falls on Christmas Eve
candlelight glows more warmly
and starshine feels more homely...
There's a touch of family 'round me
whether Bing Crosby dreamt me home
or not.

Sleigh bells jingle, and I'm listening
sparkle silver, gold, and glist'ning...
Bright. Tolling. Twinkling.
There's something lovely in the lights
when night falls on Christmas Eve.

Watch for more titles from Night Wolf Publications in 2011. Paranormal romance, steampunk, fantasy, adventure, young adult, and more will be available in print and electronic formats. Bookmark the www.nightwolfpublications.com website and learn about our authors on our facebook page.

May you have a peaceful and prosperous new year.

www.ingramcontent.com/pod-product-compliance
Lightning Source LLC
Chambersburg PA
CBHW020640130626
46552CB00003B/1321